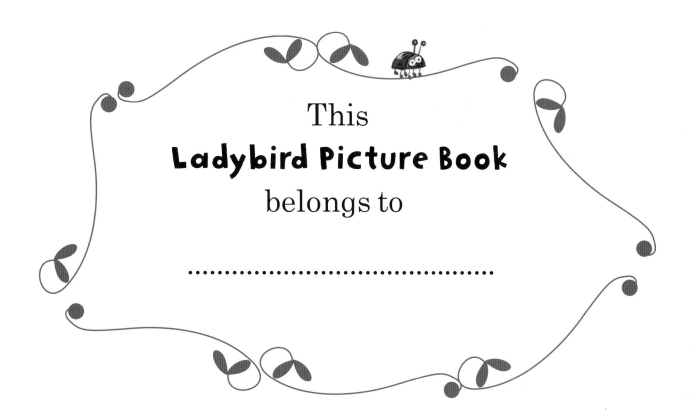

This
Ladybird Picture Book
belongs to

....

LADYBIRD BOOKS

UK | USA | Canada | Ireland | Australia
India | New Zealand | South Africa
Ladybird Books is part of the Penguin Random House group of companies
whose addresses can be found at global.penguinrandomhouse.com.

www.penguin.co.uk　　　www.puffin.co.uk　　　www.ladybird.co.uk

Penguin
Random House
UK

First published 1999
Reissued 2012 as part of the Ladybird First Favourite Tales series
This Ladybird Picture Books edition published 2018
002

Copyright © Ladybird Books Ltd, 1999, 2012, 2018

Printed in China
A CIP catalogue record for this book is available from the British Library

ISBN: 978–0–241–38793–1

All correspondence to:
Ladybird Books, Penguin Random House Children's
80 Strand, London WC2R 0RL

MIX
Paper from
responsible sources
FSC® C018179

Ladybird Picture Books

Jack and the Beanstalk

BASED ON A TRADITIONAL FOLK TALE

retold by Iona Treahy ★ illustrated by Ailie Busby

Once there was a boy called Jack who lived
with his mother. They were so poor that she
said to him one day, "We'll have to sell our
cow – it's the only way."

On the way, Jack met a stranger.
"I'll give you five beans for that cow,"
he said. "They're magic beans..."
"Done!" said Jack.
But when he got back...

"Five beans for our cow?" cried his mother.
And she threw them out of the window.

All through the night, a beanstalk grew...
and grew... till it was right out of sight.

Before his mother could say a word, Jack
climbed... and climbed... and he didn't stop
till he reached...

...the top. There, Jack saw a giant castle. He knock-knock-knocked, and a giantess opened the door.

Inside, Jack could hear a thumping and a banging and a stamping and a crashing.

What a noise!

"Quick," said the giantess.
"Hide! My husband is hungry!"

"Fee, fi, fo fum! Watch out everyone, **HERE I COME!**" roared the giant.

The giant sat down for his supper.
He ate one hundred boiled potatoes and
one hundred chocolate biscuits. And then,
feeling a bit happier, he got out his gold.

The giant started counting his coins,
but soon... he was snoozing.

Jack snatched the gold and raced down
the beanstalk.
"Gold!" cried Jack's mother when she saw
what he'd got. "We're not poor any more!"

But Jack wanted to go back up the beanstalk.
The next day he climbed... and climbed...
and he didn't stop till he reached the top.

Inside the castle, Jack hid when he heard...

a thumping and a banging
and a stamping and a crashing.

"Fee, fi, fo fum! Watch out everyone, **HERE I COME!**" roared the giant.

The giant sat down for his supper. He ate two hundred baked potatoes and two hundred jellies. And then, feeling a bit happier, he got out his hen that laid golden eggs.

The hen started laying, but soon...
the giant was snoozing. Jack snatched
the hen and raced down
the beanstalk.

"Golden eggs from a golden hen!" cried Jack's mother. "Now we'll never be poor again!"

The next day, Jack climbed the beanstalk once more.

"Fee, fi, fo fum! Watch out everyone, **HERE I COME!**" roared the giant.

The giant sat down for his supper. He ate three hundred roast potatoes and three hundred cream cakes. And then, feeling a bit happier, he got out his golden harp.

The harp sang him lullabies, and soon...
the giant was snoozing. Jack snatched the
harp and raced down the beanstalk.

But the harp called out, "Master! Master!"
The giant woke up and started to chase
after Jack.

"Bring the axe, Mother!" shouted Jack as he neared the ground. Then he chopped and he chopped and didn't stop till... CRASH! Down came the beanstalk and the giant.

And with the gold and the harp and the eggs and the hen, Jack and his mother were never poor again.

Ladybird Picture Books

Look out for...

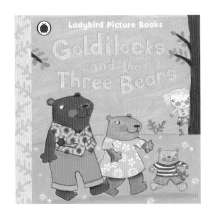

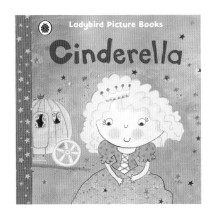

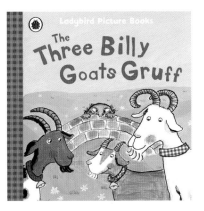

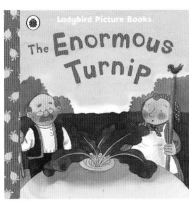

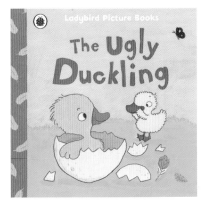

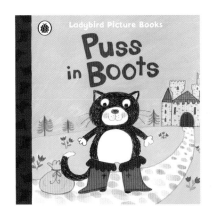